Sam's Special Cookie

Joan Evans Hartman

Illustrated by Jessica Lane Baker

Hartbeat Books
Ripley, Tennessee

For the children in Hickman County. Keep on reading!

Joan Evans Hartman

To
Scott, Evans, and Lane

Publisher's Acknowledgement

The publisher wishes to acknowledge and thank Lanzer's Printing in Union City, Tennessee for the generous advice and assistance in seeing this publication become a reality. Special thanks to Kay Roberts Smith for her advice and encouragement.

Sam's Special Cookie

Text copyright 2004 by Joan Evans Hartman

Published by   Hartbeat Books
               111 Lankford Drive
               Ripley, Tennessee 38063

First Edition 2005

Published and printed in the United States of America

Hartbeat Books ISBN Number: 0-9762515-2-3

Library of Congress Control Number: 2005920235

FORWARD

For many years I loved teaching kindergarten and first grade children. It is a special joy to have Jessica Baker, one of my former first grade students, as the illustrator of the book.

This book is based on a true life experience. I always have enjoyed having children come to my house. A few years ago Sam, the main character in the book, came "trick-or-treating" on Halloween and received what he called his "special cookie." What happens in the story offers a lesson to all who read it.

Mike Shoulders, who is also a writer of children's books, heard about this book and suggested that I should include the recipe for the "special cookie." I have included it here for you mothers, grandmothers, and teachers who would like to bake them!

Jo Jo's Special Cookies

3/4 c. soft margarine or butter
1 c. sugar
2 eggs
1 t. vanilla

2 3/4 c. flour
1 t. baking powder
1/2 t. salt

Beat together margarine, sugar, eggs, and vanilla. Mix flour, baking powder, and salt and add to other ingredients. Chill one hour. Roll out small amounts of dough. Cut in shapes and bake on greased cookie sheets at 375° for 8-10 minutes. Ice with "store bought" icing.

Special thanks to my "children"...Scott Hartman, Evans Hartman, and Lane McKinney...for their love and support and to Kay Smith, a fellow author of children's books, for her mentoring and encouragement in writing this book.

A portion of the sale of each of these books will go to St. Jude Children's Hospital in Memphis, Tennessee.

On Halloween night

He rang the bell;

Who was this calling?

It was hard to tell!

Then I saw his Mom
And Grandmother, too!
It was my friend Sam. . .
All at once I knew!

Jack-o-lantern treats
Were there on the tray
For each girl and boy
Who might come my way.

All iced in orange,

The cookie surprise

Had chocolate mouth,

A nose, and two eyes.

Sam chose his cookie
And said "Thank you!", too,
For his little treat
From the friend he knew.

He put it right in

His trick-or-treat pack

With "goodies" he found

Up my street and back.

'Twas later that night
When Sam's Mother said
"You've had lots of fun. . .
Time to go to bed."

Sam went on to sleep;

Still later that night

Sam's Mother was hungry...

She wanted a bite.

Quietly she walked
Past Sam's little bed,
Not to get candy
But COOKIE instead!

Early next morning
Sam called from his bed
"Where is my COOKIE?
I want it!" he said.

His Mom had to tell

The thing she had done;

She wanted to hide!

She wanted to run!

Sam started to cry. . .

His Grandmother knew

His Mother was wrong

And fussed at her, too!

His Mother called Jo Jo,
The friend who had baked
The special cookie
For which his heart ached.

"Today I'm leaving,
Sam will have to wait;
When I get back home,
He'll have a big plate."

To keep her promise
And honor Sam's wish,
Jo Jo baked cookies
And filled a whole dish.

The lesson is this. . . .

Forever to hear. . . .

Don't take anything

From one far or near.